Give My Regrets
to Broadway

Chet Gecko Mysteries

And coming soon

Give My Regrets
to Broadway

FROM THE TATTERED CASEBOOK OF

CHET GECKO
PRIVATE EYE

Bruce Hale

HARCOURT, INC.

Orlando • Austin • New York • San Diego • Toronto • London

Requests for permission to make copies of any part of
the work should be mailed to the following address:
Permissions Department, Harcourt, Inc.,
6277 Sea Harbor Drive, Orlando, Florida 32887-6777.

www.HarcourtBooks.com

Library of Congress Cataloging-in-Publication Data
Hale, Bruce.
Give my regrets to Broadway: from the tattered casebook
of Chet Gecko, private eye/Bruce Hale.
p.   cm.
"A Chet Gecko Mystery."
Summary: Chet and his partner, Natalie Attired, take on
a case involving an actor gone missing from
the school musical.
[1. Geckos—Fiction.   2. Plays—Fiction.
3. Schools—Fiction.   4. Animals—Fiction.   5. Mystery
and detective stories.   6. Humorous stories.]   I. Title.
PZ7.H1295Gi   2004
[Fic]—dc22   2003019440
ISBN 0-15-216700-5

Text set in Bembo
Display type set in Elroy
Designed by Ivan Holmes

C E G H F D

Printed in the United States of America

For Glynnis, Miles, Beckett, Bailey, and Rebecca

A private message from the private eye ...

To snoop or not to snoop. . . .

That's no question. Whether it's smarter to let sleeping dogs lie or to plunge in and follow a clue, I always do the same thing: Follow the clue.

Of course, you'd expect no less from Chet Gecko, Emerson Hicky Elementary's top gecko detective. (Yeah, so I'm the school's *only* gecko detective. What of it?)

My investigations have led me into situations scarier than a midnight plunge in a shark's Jacuzzi. I've chuckled at danger, giggled at doom, and snorted (gently) at catastrophe.

But when the fickle finger of fate flicked me into show business, I felt as nervous as a blindfolded brontosaurus on a high wire.

It's not that I get stage fright—the boards themselves don't scare me. But I *am* afraid of making a fool of myself *on* them.

Truth is, I'd much rather tangle with a criminal mastermind than sing and dance. But did my teacher care? Not a bit. Mr. Ratnose cast me in his dumb musical anyway.

So it was almost a relief when, right from the start, our school play took a jump into jeopardy. *Mysteries I can handle,* I thought.

But as curtain time neared, I had more close calls than a hippo on a tricycle. Many times, it looked like curtains for this gecko. I wondered whether I would die offstage or on, but then I learned something about acting that bucked me up:

Acting is all about honesty. If you can fake that, you've got it made.

1

Strike up the Bland

It was the first rehearsal for our play, and I wished I was at the dentist. Or staked to an anthill with red fire ants crawling up my nose. Or even on the losing end of a parent-teacher conference.

Anywhere but the auditorium.

Still, there I was—the last one into the building where the entire fourth grade waited. Given the choice, I'd rather pull the whiskers off a werewolf than perform in a dorky play like *Omlet, Prince of Denver.* But who had a choice?

The auditorium (or cafetorium, as the principal calls it) buzzed like a nest of baby rattlesnakes on Christmas morning. My teacher, Mr. Ratnose, huddled onstage with the other teachers. My fellow students fidgeted on the rows of wooden benches, jabbering amongst themselves.

Something was up.

I scanned the crowd. My partner and friend, Natalie Attired, had saved me a spot in the second-to-last row. Good ol' Natalie.

With a little luck, I could slip into place before Mr. Ratnose noticed my tardiness. Bending low, I hurried toward my seat. Just a few more steps . . .

I didn't see the foot in my path, but I sure felt it.

Ba-dump!

"Whoa!" I stumbled and staggered like a Rottweiler on Rollerblades.

Ka-flump! I sprawled in the aisle, flat on my face.

The room fell silent with worry.

"Haw-haw-haw!" burst from a hundred throats.

Or maybe they were just catching their breath.

I got up and brushed myself off, scowling at the guilty foot's owner—a chubby chipmunk. He smiled back as sweetly as a big brother with a carload of water balloons.

And then my bad luck multiplied.

Mr. Ratnose stepped to the edge of the stage. "Chet Gecko," he said, "even though you're tardy, I'm giving you an honor that many students dream of."

"You're letting me out of this dumb play?" I asked.

The kids giggled again. Mr. Ratnose glared at them, pricklier than a hedgehog's hug.

"Wrong," he huffed. "Our lead actor, Scott Freeh, has disappeared."

My ears perked up. (As much as two holes in your head can perk.) A missing persons case?

I trotted up the aisle. "You want me to find him, right?"

"Wrong again," said my teacher. "I'd like you to take on Scott's role."

"Me?"

"You."

"Thanks, but no thanks. I'm a private eye, not a hambone."

Mr. Ratnose crossed his arms. "Be that as it may. You will play the part, or you will write a fifty-four-page report on French classical theater."

He sure knew how to put the screws to a guy. The only thing I like less than looking foolish on-stage is writing fifty-four-page reports (although math class and lima-bean pie are right up there).

I sighed. "Okay, I'll do it. Out of curiosity, what's the part?"

His black eyes sparkled, and a smile tweaked his ratty lips. "The lead: Omlet, Prince of Denver. You've got a dramatic duet with a ghost..."

"Swell," I said.

"A swashbuckling sword fight..."

"Not bad."

"And a romantic song with Azalea that ends in a kiss."

"That's—Wait a minute! A *kiss*!?"

Mr. Ratnose nodded. "Yes, you fourth graders should be mature enough to handle that by now."

My stomach churned and tumbled like a dingo in a washing machine. Sweat turned my palms into the Okefenokee Swamp.

"Wh-who plays Azalea?" I choked out.

"Why, Shirley, of course."

My mind spun. A lip-lock with Shirley Chameleon, Smooch Monster and Cootie Queen of the Known Universe? *Yikes!* In fact, *double* yikes.

"Well, what are you waiting for?" asked Mr. Ratnose. "Get up here and rehearse."

Right then, I gave myself a new case. I would find Scott Freeh before our play opened, or my name isn't Chet "Too Young to Be Smooched" Gecko.

2

Through Thick and Twin

Before you lose your lunch, let me reassure you: I didn't have to kiss Shirley that morning. We just read the play.

The kids who weren't acting got stage crew duty. They met in a corner with Ms. Bona Petite, the teacher in charge of scenery and stage props. What a happy bunch—knowing they'd get to play with hammers, saws, and paint.

Too bad I couldn't join them.

Instead, I sat with the cast and listened to Mr. Ratnose blather on about the meaning of the play, and how he'd improved on Shakespeare's *Hamlet*.

"You'll notice," said Mr. Ratnose, "that not only have I made it a musical, which Shakespeare probably wished *he'd* thought of..."

Ms. Petite sniffed and rolled her eyes.

"But I've also given it a happy ending." Mr. Ratnose beamed at us. "That way, no first graders in the audience will get nightmares."

Igor Beaver, a championship nerd, raised his paw. "Teacher, will we be wearing tights and doublets, like the actors of Shakespeare's time?"

Mr. Ratnose's tail curled happily. I could almost see the brownie points piling onto Igor's permanent record.

"Yes, Igor," he said. "We'll use traditional costumes."

Great. Now I'd have to wear sissy tights while frolicking around the stage like a doofus. Would the torture never stop?

Miraculously, it did. After we read through the play, the recess bell rang, and our teachers dismissed us. I buttonholed Natalie Attired for some sleuthing.

Did I mention already that Natalie, my mockingbird pal, is as sharp as a pocketful of pins (but without the annoying tendency to stick into your fingers)? She is. But she does have other irritating habits.

"Hey, Chet," she said, as we watched kids milling about. "Do you know why gorillas have such big nostrils?"

"Why?"

"Because they have such big fingers!" She cackled. See what I mean?

I took Natalie by the shoulders. "Birdie, this is no time for jokes. We've got to find Scott Freeh, and pronto—so he can take back his stupid role."

"You don't want to play Omlet?" she asked. "It's such a great part."

"*I don't care.*" I fumed. "I'd rather gargle with a skunk's bathwater than kiss Shirley Chameleon. Are you gonna help me or what?"

She held up her wings. "All right, don't get grouchy. I'll help."

"Great. First we need to know what Scott looks like."

"Easy-peasy," she said. "He looks just like that." She pointed to a skinny anole lizard beside Ms. Petite.

"Huh?"

"That's Scott's twin, Bjorn."

I straightened my hat. "Twin, eh? Let's start with him."

As we approached, Bjorn Freeh was just finishing up with Ms. Petite, a ground squirrel who put the *ooh* in *ooh-la-la.*

Every school has a teacher like this. All the boys love her, and all the girls want to be like her. Ms. Bona Petite had lustrous eyes deep enough to back-stroke in, a face cuter than a box of bunnies, and a way of making you believe you were the only one in the world that mattered.

Not that I fell for any of that.

She touched Bjorn's arm. "Be strong," she said. Then she patted her jaunty cap and wafted off like expensive perfume on a summer breeze.

"You Bjorn?" I asked the anole.

He tore his gaze away from the ground squirrel and blinked at us. "Uh?"

"I'll take that as a yes."

Natalie chimed in. "What were you two discussing?"

"Oh, um, my brother's disappearance," he said.

"Funny," I said. "That's our favorite subject, too."

I sized up Bjorn. He had a tail as long as a third grader's Christmas list, and a head as flat as a frying pan.

Mmm, frying pan . . . termite crisps . . . My eyes glazed over with visions of lunch.

"So?" said Bjorn.

Regretfully, I reined in my appetite. "We need to find your brother," I said.

"ASAP," said Natalie. "Before *he*"—she pointed at me—"has to play Omlet."

"But it's such a great part," said Bjorn.

"Never *mind* the part," I said. "Where the heck is your brother?"

"He's gone," said the anole. "That's what *disappeared* means."

I clenched my teeth. "Thanks for the vocabulary lesson. But where did he go? Why? For how long?"

Bjorn started out the cafeteria door. We followed him onto a playground where kids swarmed like bees at a honey hoedown.

"Well . . . he didn't come home yesterday," said Bjorn. "But it's no big deal."

"No big deal?" I said. "Aren't your parents flipping out?"

The lizard idly fiddled with his tail. "Nah. Scott comes and goes all the time."

I sidestepped a pair of toads playing leapfrog. You get that a lot from toads.

"But I thought twins were supposed to be inseparable," said Natalie.

Bjorn shrugged. "Sure," he said. "We're as inseparable as oil and water."

"Could some enemy have kidnapped him?" I asked.

"No way," said Bjorn. "Everybody likes Scott."

"Did he get stage fright and vamoose?" asked Natalie.

The anole chuckled. "Yeah, right."

"What do you mean?" I said.

Bjorn contemplated a nearby gnat. But before he could move on it, I shot out my tongue and slurped it up. You snooze, you lose.

The lizard shot me a glance. "Look, my bro's got

ice in his veins. That's why he's such a hot soccer player. He's got stage fright like you've got an eating problem."

"But I don't have any problems eating," I said.

"Exactly."

"What?"

"Skip it," said Bjorn.

I sucked in my gut and mulled over his words.

We had reached the rusty tangle of pipes and slides that passes for playground equipment at Emerson Hicky. Bjorn gazed at the jungle gym.

"Can you think of anything to help us find your brother?" I asked.

The anole squinched up his face. "Um . . . nope," he said. "But he'll show up."

And with that, he trotted off to play.

"Hmm," I said.

"You took the hum right out of my mouth," said Natalie.

I scratched my chin. "Anything strike you as funny?"

"Yeah," she said. "Pies in the kisser, knock-knock jokes, and that face you make when you eat broccoli by mistake."

I looked at her. "Besides all that."

"Well, Bjorn didn't seem too worried about Scott's disappearance."

"He didn't, did he?"

Natalie cocked her head. "So, what does that mean?"

"Partner," I said, "the plot has officially thickened."

She grinned. "Great! Add some potato bugs and we've got a stew."

3

Soccer Puppet

It was lunchtime before Natalie and I could get back to sleuthing. After savoring the cafeteria's dwarf-spider stew and blowfly pie, I was ready to roll (but slowly, thanks to seconds on the pie).

As Natalie and I were leaving the building, I glanced at the stage. Someone had already taped up a sign:

COMING SOON:
OMLET, PRINCE OF DENVER!
A finger-lickin' good musical!

I shuddered.

From a nearby table, Tony Newt saluted me.

"Yo, Omlet," he said. "Are you the kind with mushrooms or green peppers?"

His tablemates guffawed.

"Yo, Tony," I said. "Did you know that if brains were dynamite, you couldn't blow your nose?"

I grabbed Natalie and scooted out the door. "The sooner we find Scott, the better," I said.

"What, tired of being a hot actor?"

"It ain't the heat," I said. "It's the humility."

We decided to visit Scott's teacher and pump her for clues. Turned out she was Bona Petite, school glamour-puss. We found her on yard duty.

Ms. Petite stood, chatting with a couple of girls, in the eye of a hurricane of followers. Around her, show-off boys whirled and cartwheeled and jabbered.

The playground was littered with broken hearts.

Natalie and I slipped through the ring of admirers.

"Ms. Petite," I said, "can you spare a moment?"

Her gaze, soft and sweet as a chocolate river, poured over me. With a smile meant just for me, Ms. Petite said, "Certainly."

"It's about your student Scott Freeh," said Natalie.

"Yes?" said the chic ground squirrel.

"Well, he *is* missing," I said. "We thought you might know something."

Bona Petite toyed with her fancy hat. "Poor Scottie." She sighed. "Such a talented boy..."

The girls beside her made sad faces and sighed, too.

Natalie cocked her head. "Why would he disappear? Could someone have snatched him?"

"I'm afraid I don't know," said Ms. Petite. "The office had no explanation; there was no note from home..." She shrugged. "It's a sad, sad mystery."

Her gal pals shrugged, too.

"Oh, knock it off," I said.

"What?" said Bona Petite.

"Did Scott have enemies?" asked Natalie. "Was anybody mad at him?"

"No, he— Just a moment," said Ms. Petite. "I've thought of something."

She put a paw to her cheek. Her little shadows started to follow suit, looked at me, and thought better of it.

"Yes?" said Natalie.

"The soccer players . . ."

"What about them?" I said.

"They weren't too happy when Scott quit the team to be in Mr. Ratnose's silly little play."

Natalie and I exchanged a glance.

"Ah . . . ," I said.

"Ha!" said Natalie.

"As we . . ."

"Suspected," she said.

Ms. Petite's fudge brown eyes went wide. "Was that helpful?" she asked.

I tipped my hat. "That, my dear Ms. Petite, is what we detectives call a lead."

Natalie chipped in. "And where it leads, we follow."

"You follow me?" I asked the teacher.

"I thought we were supposed to follow the lead," said Natalie.

It didn't take a Sherlock Holmes to locate the soccer players at lunchtime. If you guessed that we found them on the soccer field, give yourself a gold star.

When we arrived, a dozen or so sweaty kids were scrimmaging, kicking a beat-up ball around the grass. Natalie and I stopped on the sidelines.

"Let me handle this," I said. "It takes finesse."

"You, all finesse-y?" she said. "This I gotta see."

I stepped onto the field. "Hey, soccer jocks! Seen Scott Freeh today?"

Foom! The ball whizzed at my head.

I ducked. My hat didn't.

As I picked up my battered fedora, a bowlegged weasel trotted over. She kicked the ball back to her teammates. "Whatcha want with that loser?" she snarled.

"Scott's missing," I said. "We're trying to find him."

"Yeah? He can stay lost," said the weasel.

"Didn't you like him?" I asked.

Bam!

"*Oof!*" Something whacked me in the back and sent me sprawling. I pushed up off the grass and saw the ball bouncing merrily away. Sneaky soccer players.

The weasel snickered. "Some free advice, Gecko. If you value your health, don't talk about that traitor around here."

"Traitor?" asked Natalie.

A chuckwalla built like a refrigerator stopped the ball. "Yeah," he growled. "Dat punk dropped soccer for a stupit play."

The big reptile advanced, bouncing the ball off the tops of his feet. His teammates drifted over.

"Yeah? Then why'd Scott disappear on the first day of rehearsal?" I asked.

"Dunno," said the chuckwalla. He tapped the ball higher and higher, off his knees now. "Maybe he's outta his *head!*"

And with that, he bounced the soccer ball— *whap!*—off his forehead and—*whump!*—right into my gut.

I staggered back onto Natalie. We went down like a lead-bottomed duck.

The soccer players cackled till they choked.

"Good one, Frankie," said the weasel.

"T'anks, Angie." The chuckwalla chuckled.

Wiping away tears of laughter, they reclaimed the ball and trotted back onto the field. Natalie and I picked ourselves up.

"That finesse worked well," she said, brushing grass from her feathers.

"It's a gift," I said.

"Really?" said Natalie. "Then I think you might wanna return it."

4

For Better or Rehearse

The rest of the day flew by like a steel-winged moth with arthritis. I didn't learn much about the case at recess, and I didn't learn a danged thing in Mr. Ratnose's class. (Of course, that's not unusual.)

The last bell rang. Time for another rehearsal. Oh, joy.

I dragged my heels. By the time I reached the auditorium, my classmates were inside, but a pack of kids were milling around out front waving placards.

KEEP SHAKESPEARE PURE, read one sign. KOWS AGAINST CORNINESS, said another.

I approached the pompous pigeon who carried the second sign. "Hey, ace. What's that mean?"

"We're KOWS," he said.

"No," I said. "You're a pigeon. And she's a rabbit, and he's—"

"Not *cows*." He frowned. "KOWS."

"Right, and I'm Mother Goose."

The pigeon's grip tightened on his stick. He spoke slowly. "KOWS is Kids Opposed to Wrecking Shakespeare."

Somebody needs to get a life, I thought. But all I said was, "I see."

The rabbit cleared her throat. "We believe this play is, um, insulting to . . ."

"To all true Shakespeareans," the pigeon said.

"Really?" I said. "How now, young KOW?"

"Try this," said the bird. "How could Omlet, Prince of Denver, be a Dane? Danes are from Denmark."

I raised an eyebrow. "Methinks thou dost protest *way* too much."

The rabbit, a bedraggled bunny with a bad overbite, spoke up. "An' we're gonna keep on protesting until . . . until . . ."

"Until the school shuts the play down," said the pigeon. He quivered with indignation. "We think it's a dreadful mockery."

I nodded. "I couldn't agree more."

"Then you'll drop out of the play and join KOWS?" he said.

"Sorry," I said. "I'm not in the *moo*."

The bunny blinked. "Huh?"

My humor is wasted on most kids at this school. "Look, I've protested already," I said. "And Mr. Ratnose gave me the lead role."

The pigeon puffed himself up. "It's no joke. This play will go down, and you will go down with it."

"Probably." I wished them luck and headed inside to meet my fate.

A happy babble rang from the auditorium walls. Kids in small clusters practiced their lines. Our music teacher, Zoomin' Mayta, was a cheery hummingbird with a hyperactive sense of rhythm. She pounded out the show's theme song on an upright piano while a group sang:

> *"He's the guy who talks to ghosts:*
> *Omlet, Omlet!*
> *He's the Dane we dig the most:*
> *Omlet, Omlet!*
> *He's a good egg, that's for sure.*
> *Never cracks; he keeps it pure*
> *Even at high temperatures.*
> *Ooooh-oh-mmleeeet!"*

Onstage, Mr. Ratnose hopped and jittered about with the students playing castle guards, teaching them intricate dance moves. They stepped, they swirled, they spun.

My mouth hung open. Even to my untrained eye, they looked like Spazzmaster Flash and the Spazzmotics.

Natalie broke away from the gang at the piano.

"Hiya, Chet," she said. "Ready to make theater history?"

"I wish this play was history," I said.

Just then, one of the singers turned and glowered at me. It was the chubby chipmunk who had tripped me at the first rehearsal.

His black eyes smoldered, and the white streaks on his fat cheeks looked like racing stripes on a balloon. Nearly as wide as he was tall, the fuzzy critter looked as if he'd like nothing better than to smoosh me like a steamroller.

I pointed him out to Natalie. "Who's that mook, and what's his beef?"

"You don't recognize him?"

"No."

Natalie preened her wing feathers. "Remember Baby Boo? That TV commercial:

'Baby Boo, only two.
Watch the baby chew and chew.' "

"Yeah . . . bubble gum for babies. So what?"

"*That's* Baby Boo. Boo Dinkum."

"That lard bucket? He sure grew up. And out."

Natalie poked my gut. "Look who's talking, jelly belly."

"For your information, that's relaxed muscle. Now, why is this overgrown baby giving me the old stink-eye?"

"First," she said, "he's got a bad attitude..."

"I noticed that this morning."

"And second, you only got the lead in the play. He's been acting for years. You think he's maybe, I don't know...jealous?"

The elevator suddenly went to the top floor of my brain. "Of course. And if he really wants that part, he would've resented Scott Freeh, too."

"Enough to kidnap him?" said Natalie.

I squared my shoulders. "That, birdie, is what we're gonna find out."

But before I could take three steps, duty called. (And this time, it sounded like a lean rat with a short fuse.)

"Chet Gecko," said Mr. Ratnose, "get your tail up here and rehearse this scene."

What else could I do? My tail and I headed for the stage.

5

Chipmunky Business

I'll spare you the gory details of rehearsal. Imagine the excitement of watching a mole's nose hairs grow. Then combine that with the splendors of a visit to the lint museum. Now multiply it by the thrills of dental surgery without novocaine. . . .

You get the picture.

Things heated up while rehearsing my romantic scene with Shirley Chameleon. Although we were only supposed to be reading it, my overexcited classmate really got into her part.

When she read the line, "Oh, Omlet, you're my sweet patootie," Shirley went as pink as a six-foot stack of valentines. All in a tizzy, she leaned forward, puckering. Her lips loomed, plump and perilous.

"*Hah-choo!*" I faked an epic sneeze, spraying her with spit. Shirley backed off.

Whew.

When Mr. Ratnose finally called a break, I was raring to get back to detecting. I signaled Natalie. We cornered Boo Dinkum in the back of the room.

"What ho, young Dinkum," I said. "Prithee, tarry awhile." (A sure sign that this dumb play was getting to me.)

The chipmunk's whiskers bristled. "What do *you* want?" he said.

"A word," said Natalie.

"How 'bout *get lost*?" he sneered.

"That's two words," I said.

"Beat it."

"Still two," said Natalie.

"You . . . stay outta my face!"

I shook my head. "Aw, now you're not even trying."

The puffy rodent crossed his arms. I could tell this would be fun.

"We're after Scott Freeh," said Natalie. "Any ideas on where to look?"

His dark eyes flitted between us. "Why should *I* know?" he said. "Or care?"

"Got something against him?" I said.

The chipmunk snorted. "That clown? He couldn't act his way out of a wet paper bag." Boo looked me over. "Like some other morons I could name."

I put my hands on my hips. "Yeah? Go ahead and name 'em, bucko."

But before his mouth wrote a check his fists couldn't cash, Boo Dinkum spotted something past my left shoulder. He clammed up.

I followed his gaze. A bigger, uglier version of Boo—if that was possible—had caught Mr. Ratnose by the piano. Big Boo had a touchy temper and a face like a bucket of mud.

"What are your qualifications?" the chipmunk half shouted.

Mr. Ratnose bared his yellow teeth. "I am the director," he said. "I don't need qualifications."

"What kind of lamebrain would cast a rank amateur in a lead role when he could have an experienced actor like my son?"

Mr. Ratnose gripped the chipmunk by the elbow and led him toward the door. "If you'd rather not be a parent volunteer," he said, "just say so."

"Oh, no you don't," said the snippy rodent. "I'll be sticking around to make sure you don't give my boy an even smaller part." He stared at us as if we were something he'd scraped off his shoe. "Come along, Boo."

Boo Dinkum deflated like a bagpipe in a cactus patch. Head down, he slouched over to the door and joined his father.

Natalie nodded at the chipmunks, father and son. "Think they could've done something to Scott Freeh?"

"No doubt," I said. "But the soccer players were steamed at Scott, too. For a guy with no enemies, he's got some interesting friends."

Before we could discuss our case further, Mr. Ratnose called. "Let's do some blocking for your scenes," he said.

I frowned. "*Blocking?* Why, is someone trying to tackle me?"

Mr. Ratnose took a long breath. "*Blocking* means planning where the actors move." His whiskers looked frazzled. Either all the excitement was getting to him or my teacher needed to try a new conditioner.

We joined the group. Under Mr. Ratnose's direction, we exited and entered, walked here, stood there, and generally bopped all across the stage. After ten minutes, my legs felt like lasagna noodles and my brain felt like mush. Acting was harder than it looked.

Once, some high, mournful singing distracted me. I looked over at Natalie.

She'd heard it, too. "Wasn't me," she said.

The singing continued.

Mr. Ratnose scowled at the kids onstage, but none of them was making the sound. He stared out into the auditorium.

"Ms. Mayta," he said, "will you stop that singing?"

The hummingbird glanced up from her crossword puzzle. "What singing?"

The song had stopped.

"Very funny," said Mr. Ratnose. "People, let's save the songs for music rehearsal. We're acting now, so let's act."

We gave it a shot. But between the corny lines and the giggly crew, it was hard to focus.

Until something happened that sobered everyone up.

We were working on the scene where Omlet has breakfast with the king and queen—the queen being Natalie, and the king being a toad named Hiram. Other kids walked to and fro, pretending to serve us.

"Prithee, good Omlet, pass the butter," said Queen Natalie. (I'm not kidding, that's how we had to talk.) "This honey doth make my belly rumble."

"To be or not to be," I said. "That's indigestion."

I had leaned over to grab the pretend butter when two things happened almost at once:

Creeeak came a noise from above us; and then . . .

CRASH! fell a stage light, two inches from my tail.

6

A Midsummer Light's Scream

Glass shattered. The stage exploded in confusion. Kids jumped back, kids crowded forward. Girls (and a couple of boys) wailed like wet babies.

And me? For once, my quick gecko reflexes failed me. I stood and stared at the heavy light like I'd been turned into a statue of Doofus Maximus.

Natalie reached my side, her worried eyes big as bowls. "Are you all right?"

"Gaa," I finally managed. "Gaa go gee." I pointed at the hunk of black metal and broken glass.

"You said it," she said.

I found my voice. "Another few inches, and it would've crushed my tail."

"Or your head," said Natalie.

"That's my least vulnerable spot," I said. But a chill danced a mambo down my spine, nevertheless.

After making sure I was okay, Mr. Ratnose checked out the light. "I don't know how this could have fallen," he said. He fumbled with the bracket that had attached the fixture to a pipe up above. "Strange...," he said.

"What?" I asked.

"The bracket didn't break, and the screws that held it together are missing."

"Which means?" said Natalie.

The rat shook his head. "Somebody deliberately... No, I can't believe it."

"You mean...?" My blood sizzled like triple-strength espresso. "Someone tried to take me out?"

Natalie and I exchanged a glance.

"*Mm,* and they might still be up there," said Hiram the toad.

We all gazed at the network of pipes and stage lights that hung from the ceiling. Dark shadows lurked behind the lights. They could hide anything—from a skulking bad guy to a bunch of bats playing patty-cake.

Still buzzing from shock, I acted without thinking. (Okay, it wasn't the first time.) I leaped onto the moth-eaten blue curtains. Up, up, up I scrambled.

"Chet," called Natalie, "be careful!"

At the top, I paused and surveyed the space. Nothing moved. Nobody home but us geckos.

Below me, a long way down, upturned faces watched my progress.

"What do you see?" shouted Natalie.

Swirling dust tickled my nose. "Nothing yet."

I latched on to a pipe and shinnied out toward where the light had hung, carelessly singeing my tail on another fixture.

Yikes! I almost lost my grip. But I kept crawling.

"Well?" called Natalie.

A clear space showed in the dust where the bracket had been.

With a flap and a flutter, Natalie flew up and landed on the pipe beside me. "Leave your partner in suspense, why don't you," she said.

"Swell," I said. "You just erased any prints."

She winced. "Oops. Hey, check that out."

A narrow ledge jutted beside the pipe, some kind of catwalk. Natalie was pointing at something on the walkway. Three screws. Well, well.

We climbed onto the catwalk and spotted scuff marks in the dust. They led along the ledge and ended at a ladder.

"Great. *Now* I find the easy way up," I said.

"Maybe someone removed the screws, ducked

down the ladder, and went out the back door," said Natalie.

My eyes traced the route. "And in the confusion, nobody would've noticed."

"Or," she said, cleaning dust from her feathers, "it could just be the paw prints of whoever hung the lights here."

I edged to the ladder and began climbing down.

"Either way, this whole thing stinks like rancid centipede stew," I said. "And you and I, partner, are gonna get to the bottom of it."

"Eew," she said. "Of the rancid stew?"

"No, ding-dong. Of the mystery."

Honestly. Some birds.

7

No Business Like Crow Business

The cast's concentration had shattered along with the fallen light—even Mr. Ratnose had to admit it. He canceled the rest of rehearsal.

Natalie and I headed to my house for a restorative snack. Nothing like a brush with death and dismemberment to give you an appetite, I always say.

The next day, we met by the flagpole before school. Mornings aren't my strong suit. Normally, I'd rather be torn apart by savage rhinoceros beetles than wake up early, but these weren't normal times.

My partner trilled, "What's the story, morning glory?"

I grunted.

"Aw, someone didn't eat his sunshine flakes," she said. "What's wrong?"

"It's morning," I grumped. "What else?"

Natalie held up a wing. "I can make you smile. Knock-knock."

I just stared, but she wouldn't give up. "Oh, all right. Who's there?"

"Interrupting cow," she said.

"Interrupting co—"

"Moo."

"Ha, ha, that's—"

"Moo," she said again.

"Okay, Nata—"

"Moo."

I narrowed my eyes. "I think you've milked that one long enough."

"My jokes are an udder disaster." She sighed and, mercifully, dropped it.

We worked our way through the parade of parents leaving their kids at the curb. The office windows glowed like radioactive cheese patties. Inside, we pushed past the usual whiners, malingerers, and parents with excuse notes.

We had a date with Maggie Crow, school secretary.

The secretary is a bulldozer under a lace hankie, the thinly disguised power that runs any school. Without her, even the principal would be lost.

Maggie Crow was the mother of all secretaries.

"That's no excuse note," she squawked at a mama Chihuahua. "That's a major work of fiction. If little Tiffany was sick, how come she's tanned?"

The mother blushed and hustled little Tiffany away.

I slapped a friendly grin onto my kisser. Although Mrs. Crow was hard on fakes and phonies, she had a soft spot in her heart for detectives.

"What's cookin', brown eyes?" I said.

"Not you again," she said.

See what I mean?

"We're looking for Scott Freeh," I said. "Got anything?"

"Yeah, a hot tip."

Natalie and I exchanged a glance. A break at last!

"What's the tip?" asked Natalie.

Mrs. Crow looked down her beak at us. "Never bother a secretary between her first cup of coffee and sunset."

"But . . . that's the whole day," I said.

The secretary tapped her head. "And they told me you were slow on the uptake."

Before she could turn to the next parent, I leaned over her desk.

"A student is missing," I said. "Don't you care?"

She gave me dead eyes.

"Let me rephrase that," I said. "What would it take to make you care?"

A minute later, we'd exchanged the pledge of a night-crawler pie for some information. It turned out that Scott's teacher was right—his parents hadn't sent an excuse note to the office.

"And when I called 'em, they said Scott wasn't missing," said Mrs. Crow. "They told me he went to school, same as usual."

Natalie cocked her head. "But he's *not* here," she said.

"It ain't my problem," squawked the crow. "It's the truant officer's. Now step aside; I'm a busy bird."

We left with as many questions as we'd come in with—something that usually happened only in Mr. Ratnose's class. Hashing it over, we ambled.

"You get the feeling something's fishy?" I asked.

"Yup," said Natalie, "but I can't figure it trout."

I groaned. "Just for the halibut," I said, "let's assume someone is lying."

And before Natalie could try to top my pun, someone let out a *psst.*

"Want some more beans with your birdseed?" I said.

Natalie stopped. "Wasn't me. It came from there." She pointed to the corner of the building.

We poked our heads around it and saw what appeared to be another building. But this one looked mean.

I blinked. In the shadows stood a beetle-browed

badger. He wasn't quite as tall as the Eiffel Tower, and his shoulders weren't as broad as the Rockies. But still you could tell: When this guy sat around the house, he sat *around* the house.

"C'mere," he grunted.

We kept a wary distance. "The view's better from over *here*," I said. "So what's goin' down, aside from your IQ?"

The badger growled like a thunderstorm in a subway tunnel. But when his voice emerged, it was thick as frozen peanut butter and surprisingly high.

"Dude, I got a message," he said.

"Really?" I said. "Is it a singing telegram, or were you gonna say it with flowers?"

"Huh?" he grunted.

I could tell we were moving too fast for him. But even a crippled snail would be too swift for this musclehead.

"What's the message?" asked Natalie.

"Stop it," he said.

"That's it?" she said. "Just *stop it*?"

He gnawed his lip with a fang like a stalactite. He searched his mind. It was a long, long tour of an empty cave. Finally, the badger said, "Yeah."

"Stop what?" I asked. "Playing hopscotch on the railroad tracks?"

"Making bad jokes that kids don't get?" asked Natalie.

The big lug's eyebrows met like caterpillar wrestlers. "Y' know...stop...looking for the missing dude, dude."

"You mean Scott?" I said.

"Uh, yeah."

This badger was no Einstein. In fact, the League of Barking-Mad Morons could sue him for giving morons a bad name.

He hadn't hatched this idea on his own.

"Who asked you to send the message?" I said, trying the direct approach.

The badger waved a wicked claw as long as a cavalry sword. "Ah-ah-ah. The furry one said don't tell."

Not as dumb as he looked, this badger. (But not by much.)

"Anything else?" asked Natalie.

The badger grinned. "Yeah," he said. In a flash, he swung a fistful of claws and took a chunk out of the building. "You should take me serious."

I backed up. "Serious as a summer without vacation," I said.

He growled.

Even a bad actor recognizes his cue. We took ours and bowed out.

8

The Diva Made Me Do It

Morning rehearsal was as hard to escape as that funky-smelling aunt who always wants to hug you at holiday parties. It was no use resisting (and Mr. Ratnose knew all my hiding places, anyway), so I went along.

Outside the auditorium, the demonstrators marched—more numerous than yesterday. And burlier, too. I noticed some broad-shouldered beefcakes that didn't look like poetry lovers. Didn't these goofballs have classes to attend?

Several protesters bumped and shoved the cast members as they passed. A surly bullfrog menaced Shirley Chameleon with his KOWS sign.

She hooked his feet with her curly tail, pulled,

and sent the goon sprawling. The sign hit his head with a hard *thwock!*

The frog should've known better. Don't mess with a diva.

Shirley flounced through the doors. I made to follow her, and a familiar bowlegged weasel blocked my way: Scott's teammate Angie, the soccer player.

"Not so fast," she sneered.

"Okay," I said. "How 'bout if I walk reeeeally slooowwwly?"

The weasel loved my wit. I could tell by her clenched jaw and laser gaze.

"Since when have you been acting in stupid plays, detective?" she asked.

"Since when have you cared about Shakespeare, jockette?"

She pouted. "Jockettes can like Shakespeare, too. His movies are, um, killer-diller. And this play, uh, does bad stuff to his, um, work."

I tilted my head. "Uh-huh. Tell me, who put you up to this?"

"What do you mean?" she asked.

"You don't give two toots about Shakespeare," I said. "Who told you to come wave signs with these nerds?"

"Co— Uh, no one," said the weasel.

I looked her up and down. "Okay then, who's the head of KOWS?"

"Nobody you know."

"How do you know who I know?"

She tapped her head. "Know-how."

"No," I said. "How?"

The weasel leaned close, smelling of sweat and a hint of lavender. She said, "Know what else? This play is doomed. Get out while you can."

I pushed her back and strolled into the building.

Natalie was waiting. "Wasn't that a soccer player from yesterday?"

"Maybe," I said, "but she's a KOW now."

"Wow."

"No, KOW."

"How, KOW?"

I shrugged. "How do I know? But there's something funny about them."

"Besides their name?" Natalie smoothed her shoulder feathers.

"Besides that."

She mused as we walked past groups of gabbing students. "I'm beginning to think Scott's disappearance is connected with this play," she said.

Before I could follow up on that thought, Mr. Ratnose clapped his hands. "Okay, people. Time's a-wastin'. Let's begin."

As we headed for the stage, I dug a sandwich from my pocket and started munching.

Natalie fanned her wing. *"Pee-yew!"* she said. "What's that?"

I held up my garlic-Limburger-stinkweed sandwich. "Let's call it . . . insurance."

"Call it what you want, but keep it away from me."

Rehearsal went smoothly. The songs were off-key. The dancers kept tromping on each other's feet. The acting was awful. It was as lovely to behold as a team of waltzing rhinos falling down a flight of stairs.

Boo Dinkum rolled his eyes in disgust. He exchanged looks with his father, who leaned on a wall, watching me.

Then came my big scene with Shirley Chameleon, and I forgot all about the case. My palms got clammy. My throat felt like I'd swallowed a poodle. And it wasn't just the aftertaste of the sandwich.

Shirley made goo-goo eyes. In a voice like a soap-opera queen, she said, "Oh, Omlet, you're my sweet patootie." She puckered up and aimed her bazooka lips.

"*Hahhhh,* sweet Azale*ahhh.* My main squeeze-*ahhh.*" My stink breath gushed like Old Faithful (if that geyser had smelled like a baboon's gym shorts).

Shirley's eyes watered. Her lips wilted. After a couple of coughs, she turned aside. Not even a squadron of hoochie-mamas could withstand that stench.

"Can we . . . *ack* . . . do the kiss later?" she choked out.

"How's next week?" said Mr. Ratnose. "Do you need some water, Miss Chameleon?"

Shirley nodded and stumbled toward the drinking fountain by the bathrooms at the back. I breathed a sigh of relief.

Mr. Ratnose took a step back. His long schnoz wrinkled. "What's causing that smell?" he asked.

I raised a shoulder. "In-stinked?"

Rehearsal resumed with the castle party scene. A

few minutes later, it was time for Shirley to make her entrance.

"Shirley Chameleon," said Mr. Ratnose, "it's your line."

Nothing.

"Miss Chameleon," he said, "chop-chop. You're on."

But she wasn't.

I scanned the room, feeling a little guilty.

"Maybe your stink breath sent her to the nurse's office," Natalie said.

"Ha, *hahhh,*" I said, but she fanned the fumes away.

Waldo the furball and Bosco Rebbizi searched the auditorium. They even checked outside, but Shirley was nowhere to be found.

"Darn that lizard," said Mr. Ratnose. "Isn't that just like an actress? Bitty Chu, read Shirley's part."

As the scene continued, I grew more and more uneasy.

No way would Shirley skip out on her big role. Had she disappeared like Scott Freeh?

We were working the final dance number when I got my answer. First, a weird, high singing began—quietly, then louder and louder. Just like yesterday, no one could place its source.

"M-maybe this place is haunted," said Hiram the

toad, shuddering. "And m–maybe the ghosts don't like our play."

"Nonsense!" said Mr. Ratnose. "If this auditorium is haunted, then I am the Queen of the May."

BOCK-A-DOOM!

A thunderclap rang out, and a cloud of purple smoke appeared in the middle of the stage. We coughed and backed away. As the smoke cleared, a figure emerged: a stunned and scared Shirley Chameleon.

I turned to Mr. Ratnose. "Your Majesty, would you like your crown and gown?"

9

Actions Spook Louder Than Words

The hubbub bubbled for several minutes. Some kids crowded by the doors, ready to bolt. Some pressed forward and babbled questions.

Through the smoke wisps, I saw Natalie's face. Like my own, it held a question: *What the heck is going on here?*

Finally, a rhythmic thumping cut through the noise. What fresh strangeness was this? A quick check revealed Mr. Ratnose banging an old boot on the stage.

"Settle down, everyone," he shouted.

We settled.

Mr. Ratnose advanced on Shirley. "Where did you go, young lady? And what's the idea of breaking up my rehearsal?"

Shirley shrank into herself like a homesick butter-fly returning to the cocoon.

"S-sorry," she said. "I was g-getting a drink when something grabbed me from behind and covered my mouth." She shivered.

"A ghost!" squealed Bjorn Freeh. "This play is cursed!"

Several kids gasped. "That's enough," said Mr. Ratnose, silencing them with a scowl. "Go on, Shirley. What happened next?"

She blinked. "I don't know. I felt all dizzy, a-and I blacked out. Next thing I know, something went..."

BOCK-A-DOOM! The thunderclap roared again.

"Yes, that's right," said Shirley. "And here I was."

Natalie fanned the new smoke cloud with her wings and plucked something from the heart of it.

"What's that?" I asked.

She held up a note. "Listen to this," she said.

"The play must not go on, or worse things yet will happen. This I swear by the scarlet skull.

—The Phantom
P.S. Stop the show if you want to see Scott Freeh alive again!"

"It's got my brother!" wailed Bjorn. The lizard collapsed in a faint.

A low moan rippled through the cast, like winter wind through swamp grass. If I'd had any hair, it would've stood on end.

"Well, rehearsal was just about over, anyway," said Mr. Ratnose.

The rest of the morning was pretty tame, compared to that. Mr. Ratnose gave us quiet reading time while he soothed his frayed nerves behind a book. When the recess bell buzzed, I knew just where to go.

Natalie was waiting on the steps of the library, whistling a spooky tune.

"Partner, you read my mind," I said.

"When the going gets weird...," she said.

"The weird get going... to the librarian."

Inside the air-conditioned quiet of the library sat a massive possum in a blue beret. His name was Aloyicious Theonlyest Bunk, but for reasons known only to his mom (and maybe his therapist), everyone called him Cool Beans.

Emerson Hicky's resident expert on the supernatural, Cool Beans had seen it all. He was as hard to shake as a steel magnolia tree.

"Uh-oh," he said as we approached his desk.

"Uh-oh?" I asked.

Cool Beans surveyed us from behind wrap-around shades. "Every time you cats come 'round, trouble follows. What is it this time: werewolves on the jungle gym or vampires in the cafeteria?"

"Uh, neither," I said.

"It's a ghost," said Natalie.

"Ghosts?" rumbled the possum. "Don't that just blow your gasket? Man, I guess the ghoul repellent ain't workin'. All right, lay it on me from the front."

"Um, okay." We told him about the strange doings at the auditorium—the eerie singing, the crashing light, the note, and Shirley's dramatic re-appearance.

"So, what do you think?" I asked.

"Weirdsville," said Cool Beans, scratching his chest. "Could be a real phantom. Hard to say."

"If it is," I said, "what are we up against? Can a ghost be a kidnapper?"

For a moment, I thought he hadn't heard me. He kept staring down.

"Uh, Cool Beans?" said Natalie. "Are you trying to reach the spirits?"

"Nah." The huge possum pinched his arm. "Just the fleas."

I couldn't help him there. A gecko will eat just about any insect, but I draw the line at fleas. Too salty.

"Getting back to the ghost?" I said.

He popped the flea into his mouth. "Right you

are, daddy-o. Your typical ghost usually haunts for a reason, like . . . unfinished business."

"Okay," I said. "How far will they go?"

"Way gone," he said. "And ghosts can really wail. They can move stuff, make loud noises, give a mean wedgie—almost anything a person can do."

Natalie ruffled her feathers. "So how do we make sure it's a ghost?"

"And then," I said, "how do we get rid of it?"

"You exorcise it," said Cool Beans.

I raised an eyebrow. "Right. Because . . . ghosts are afraid of jumping jacks?"

"Actually, sit-ups are scarier," said Natalie.

"Not exercise, *exorcise*," said the possum. He leaned onto his thick forearms. "You drive it out with a ritual ceremony."

"I knew that," I said.

Natalie smirked.

"And if the hullabaloo stops after the exorcism, you had a ghost," the librarian said. He leaned back.

"And if it doesn't stop?" asked Natalie.

"Then," said Cool Beans, "you got a real problem."

10

In the Nick of Slime

We decided to leave the exorcising for later, and try detect-orcising first. All through lunchtime, Natalie and I chased down leads and looked for Scott Freeh.

No dice. He was as well hidden as a principal's sense of humor.

The school day rolled by in the usual way. (Slow and excruciating, like a nostrilectomy performed with a plastic butter knife.)

Just before the last bell, Cassandra the Stool Pigeon raised her wing. "Mr. Ratnose," she asked, "do we have to keep on rehearsing the play?"

Our teacher's ears went pink. "Of course," he said. "The show must go on."

My classmates exchanged worried looks. The ship was sinking, but this rat wasn't about to desert it.

It was a somber group that met in the auditorium a few minutes later. Muttering kids checked backstage for ghostly signs. Waldo the furball jumped at every little sound. Girls tried to comfort a troubled Bjorn Freeh.

Mr. Ratnose finally corralled the group's attention. "People, we won't let these little scare tactics derail our play. Will we?"

A couple of kids nodded. Hiram the toad said, "Uh, maybe?"

That wasn't the response my teacher wanted. "Come, come," he said, forcing a chuckle. "There's no ghost. Someone is trying to stifle artistic expression."

Waldo raised his hand. "Maybe we should let them," he said.

"Tut-tut. Are you an actor or a mouse?" asked Mr. Ratnose.

Actually, I'd been wondering that myself. No one knew exactly what kind of animal Waldo was.

The furball shrugged. "Is there a third choice?"

Mr. Ratnose harrumphed. He abandoned the pep talk, sorted us into lines, and began rehearsing the big dance number, "D Is for Denver."

Although spooked (literally), the cast followed orders. We clomped around the stage to Zoomin' Mayta's piano accompaniment. "Sing out," she cried.

We sang:

> "D is for Denver, a happy, happy place.
> E is for eggplant, you stick it in your face.
> N is for nimrods, you'll never find them here.
> V is for . . ."

I'll spare you the rest. After fifteen minutes of this nonsense, my castmates finally started to loosen up. Even Shirley Chameleon lost her haunted look.

I actually thought we might make it through a rehearsal without trouble.

Silly me.

We were just finishing the high kicks, before spelling out a huge D, when disaster reared its ugly head. Again.

It began slowly, with a serious stench. My nostrils flared at the scent of funky swamp ooze mixed with something pungent I couldn't quite place.

"Chet?" asked Natalie with a meaningful stare.

"What?" I said. "Why do you think every weird smell comes from me?"

"I dunno," she said. "Because it usually does?"

But before my wit could retaliate, we learned the true source of the stink.

With a long, drawn-out *Ssschooop!* green goop rained down from above.

Plips and plops and ropey strands fell on dancers and stage alike. It was slimy and thick, a snot storm. The floor grew slicker than a politician up for reelection.

Hiram the toad slipped on a slime patch and thudded into two dancing mice. *Ba-whonk!* They all collapsed in a heap.

Shirley Chameleon skidded onto her back and took down Waldo, Bitty Chu, and Bo Newt—*blim! blam! blom!*—like a green bowling ball with a long tail.

I hopped aside . . . right into the gunk. Scrambling, I tried to keep my balance. No use.

Oomph! I plowed straight into Mr. Ratnose's furry belly.

His eyes widened. His arms windmilled.

"Eeeeaaauugh!" We hit the stage like a warthog hits an all-you-can-eat buffet. Hard.

As I lay faceup, stunned, I caught a flash of movement behind the bright lights and last drips of slime. It vanished.

From the other direction, something white entered my sight. A paper airplane, twisting and turning in air currents. It landed softly on my belly.

I grabbed the paper and unfolded it. The scribbled note read:

See? I told you so.
—*The Phantom*

I stuffed the note into my pocket. The last thing this bunch needed was another ghostly message. I raised my head and looked around.

Green goo coated the actors and the stage. The few kids who hadn't tumbled stood on the sidelines, balancing on nervous legs.

Natalie was among them. She shook a drop of goop from a wing feather.

I waved at her. "Can you fly up and see where that mess came from?"

She eyed the ceiling. The slime had mostly stopped dripping. "Oookay," she said. "If you *really* want me to."

"I *really* do."

Natalie flapped her way up to the level of the stage lights. She hovered (not easy for a mocking-bird) while she checked things out.

"Well?" I asked, getting to my feet.

My partner glided down and landed outside the spatter zone. *"Nada,"* she said. "Nobody there, and no sign of the slime source."

My eyes widened. "You know what this means?"

She nodded. "Maybe there really is a ghost," she said.

"That, or one more possibility."

"What's that?"

I wiped slime from my cheek. "Somebody's invisible flying elephant really needs a handkerchief."

11

Badger Late Than Never

One good thing came from the slime attack: Rehearsal was canceled for the day. We all *slooshed* out of the auditorium while Maureen DeBree and her janitors tackled the lake of goo.

I retrieved my skateboard and rolled home, Natalie gliding beside me. Together, we hashed over the case.

"That's one yucky ghost," she said.

"Or a yucky ghost impersonator," I said.

"Maybe it kidnapped Scott Freeh."

"Why would it?" I shook some green goop off my sleeve and flung it onto a neighbor's rosebush as we passed. "Say a ghost *is* haunting the auditorium; what's it got against Scott?"

Natalie smirked. "Maybe they were talking and he spook out of turn."

"Well, that just ghost to show you...," I said, stopping in my driveway.

"That the phantom is too ghoul for school."

I groaned and grabbed my skateboard. "But while we're talking suspects, let's not forget the soccer players and Boo's dad."

"That's the spirit," said Natalie.

For the life of me, I couldn't think of another ghostly pun. That told me one thing for sure: It was time for a snack.

Next morning, the sun cast a rosier light on things. Or maybe the slime in my eyes had made them bloodshot. Anyway, it was Friday.

Morning rehearsal actually went smoothly for a change. I kept expecting a plague of locusts to eat the auditorium, or the walls to start bleeding spaghetti sauce, but our run-through was a slam dunk. Shirley didn't even try to kiss me.

The only disruption came from Bona Petite's stage crew outside. Their hammering and sawing got so enthusiastic, Mr. Ratnose had to ask them to keep it down.

Wielding a mighty hammer, Ms. Petite tossed her head and closed the doors.

Just before recess, Mr. Ratnose made an announcement. "I just want to commend you all on the progress you're making," he said. "In spite of the . . . er, interruptions, we're well ahead of schedule."

My fellow actors grinned and swelled like a pack of dragonfly popovers. We *were* pretty awesome, at that.

"And that's why," said the lean rat, "I've decided to move up our performance date. We open next Thursday!"

I gaped. "*Thursday?* I haven't even memorized my lines."

My teacher gave me his beady-eyed stare. "But you will," he said. "All of you will learn them over the weekend, or else."

My stomach sank like a granite doughnut in a glass of milk. I hadn't bothered learning any dialogue, as I'd expected to find Scott in plenty of time. But what if he stayed lost?

The answer came: In less than a week, I'd be wearing dorky tights and kissing Shirley Chameleon.

Sweet fancy spudsuckers! Time to kick the detecting into high gear.

The recess bell rang. Kids blasted out of the auditorium like spray from a can of cricket soda. I would've joined them, but something stopped me. My teacher.

"Just a minute," said Mr. Ratnose. His pointy kisser was unreadable.

"I'm working on my lines," I said. "Honest."

The rat folded his arms. "That's not why I wanted to talk, and you know it."

Rattled, I racked my brain for recent misdeeds. "Okay... let me say in my defense, that wasn't my whoopee cushion—no matter what Sandy says."

"Whoopee cushion?" He blinked. "I meant detective work."

"Of course! Just joking. What's the case?"

"Hmm." Mr. Ratnose stroked his whiskers. "As you've no doubt noticed, someone—or something—is trying to sabotage my play," he said. "And I won't have it. I want you to find out who's behind it all."

"I don't come cheap."

"Name your price," he said.

"Take me out of this play."

He scowled. "Not for all the cheese in Tillamook."

"Okay, then," I said. "I get a hundred bucks a day, plus expenses."

Mr. Ratnose's scowl deepened. "I happen to know you get fifty cents a day."

Drat. He was pretty sharp, for a teacher.

I lobbed the ball back into his court. "Then what's your offer?"

"You get an A in English, no matter how badly you mess up my play."

I scratched my chin. An A would go a long way with my parents. It might even get my TV privileges restored. "Fair enough," I said. "I'm on it."

We nodded at each other, and I scooted out of the building. Not bad, not bad at all—getting an A for working a case I was already on.

Happy shouts rang from the playground. My schoolmates were making the most of their brief freedom. I scanned the halls for Natalie, but she'd already flown the coop.

Figuring to find her at the swings, I started that way. But I'd only reached the corner of the building when something blotted out the sun.

"Dude, you don't listen so good," said a thick-as-peanut-butter voice.

I glanced up. The brawny badger was back.

"Look, buddy—" I said.

"How'd ya know my name?" he asked.

"Huh?"

"I'm Buddy Tookas," the big guy said.

"Yeah, and I'm Little Rabbit Foo-Foo," I said. "Now buzz off, stretch; I got places to go."

I moved to step around the big lunk. A heavy paw grabbed my shoulder.

"Unh-uh," said Buddy. "I told ya don't look for the dude, but yer still lookin' for him."

I lost all feeling in my arm. "How do you know that?"

"I know. And that means ya ain't takin' me serious." The badger's paw squeezed harder. "That's a bummer."

I gritted my teeth. "Can't you just write me a ticket, cancel my shore leave, and give me two demerits?"

The badger frowned. Too many choices. He went back to his favorite. "No," he said. "Think I'll hurt ya now."

The
bruiser
plucked me
up as easily as
picking belly-button
lint. As he clomped down
the hall, Buddy bounced me
off his knees like a soccer ball.

"Can't we—*oof*—talk about—*ow*—this?" I asked.

"No way," he said. "First, yer all 'ha ha ha.' But now *I'm* all 'ha ha ha.'"

And with that, he drop-kicked me—*foom!*—right into an overripe Dumpster.

The stench made my eyes water. The bruises made my body ache.

Buddy stuck his ugly snout over the bin. "Three things, dude," he said, holding up two fingers. "Drop the case, and this is yer last warning." And in a math-challenged moment, he was gone.

I lay there groaning, surrounded by curdled carrion-beetle chowder, sour cottage cheese, and things too foul to mention. After a while, I heard a flutter.

Natalie landed on the edge of the Dumpster.

"Stop me if I've mentioned this before," she said, "but you stink."

"Stop," I said. "And help me out."

She eyed me. "You want my help? Here's what I recommend: Learn to dress better, do your homework, and, oh yeah, take a shower every now and then."

"Gee, Natalie. I don't deserve a partner like you."

Natalie blushed. "Really?"

I sighed. "Really."

12

Bye-Bye, Banshee

They say that clothes make the man. If that's true, then what did my Dumpster-dipped outfit make me? Rodney Rancid?

Whatever the effect, at least it discouraged Shirley Chameleon from inviting me to rehearse our scenes privately. You take the small victories where you can.

Come lunchtime, I dashed through the sprinklers to wash off my *eau de garbage* odor. After a brief rest and a heaping plateful of jumping-spider goulash from the cafeteria, I was ready for anything. (Well, maybe not a ten-page spelling test, but almost anything.)

Natalie and I checked carefully for my buddy, Buddy, before we got to work. It pays to be prudent when dealing with large, angry animals.

First stop: the library. We sized up our suspects as we strolled the halls.

"Wouldn't it be handy," I said, "if there really is a phantom who kidnapped Scott and is sabotaging the play?"

"That'd make our job easier," said Natalie.

"But if it's not a real ghost, then who's playing the phantom? . . . Boo's dad? Maybe he kidnapped Scott so Boo could play Omlet."

"If that's true," said Natalie, "why hasn't he kidnapped *you*?"

"*Hmm.* Good point." We walked on.

"Maybe it's the soccer players," she said. "They abducted Scott because he quit the team. And they're sabotaging the play out of spite."

I eyed a passing mosquito. When it zigged, I zagged. *Fa-zip!* My tongue reeled it in. For this gecko, any time is snack time.

"Chet, what do you think?" asked Natalie.

I chewed. "I think it'd taste better with ketchup."

"About my theory, bug-brain."

"If the soccer players took Scott, how come they were still so ticked off when we met them?"

Natalie frowned. "Hadn't thought of that."

"But I did see some soccer players in that group of morons from KOWS," I said. "Maybe KOWS snatched him."

"He *is* full of bull," said Natalie. "But, naw, they don't seem like the type."

I scratched my head. "Then what about whoever sicced that overgrown badger on us? What did he say, 'the fuzzy one'?"

She lifted a shoulder. "This school is full of fuzzy ones."

We stopped outside the library door.

"Okeydoke . . . where does that lead us?" I asked.

"Back to the ghost," we said together. So we went inside and put a proposition to our local ghostmeister, Cool Beans.

"I dunno," the possum said. "Exorcisms ain't really my bag. Sure you don't need a reference search or a wailing kazoo solo?"

"We're sure," I said.

After I promised him a plate of my mom's apricot-glazed maggot bars, Cool Beans finally saw the light. He packed a few items, turned the library over to his assistant, and set off for the auditorium.

By the time we arrived, the lunch crowd had dribbled out. The room was dim. The odors of lemony detergent and grilled termites mingled in the air.

Cool Beans took his time setting up. (At least, I think he did. Opossums move so slowly, he could've been breaking a possum land-speed record, for all I knew.) Finally, he finished.

A circle of candles ringed the stage. Inside it lay three silk scarves, a cup of water, a small bundle of weeds, a portable cassette player, and half a nematode-on-rye sandwich.

"What's the sandwich for?" I asked.

"Me," said the huge possum. "I haven't finished lunch yet." He took a massive bite.

"Can we get on with it?" I said.

"Never hurry an exorcist," said Cool Beans. "You get sloppy exorcisms."

He put down the sandwich, picked up the weedy bundle, and hit PLAY on the boom box. Crazy bongo riffs ricocheted off the walls.

"What's *that*?" asked Natalie.

"Mood music," said the possum. "Now zip your flap and let me work."

Natalie and I gave him room.

Cool Beans lit the weeds with a pocket lighter. "Spooks don't dig sage," he confided. Waving the sage above his head, the librarian paced the stage.

"Oh, Great Cosmic Muffin, dig my sound," he crooned. "We come to cast out a subterranean spirit with a heavy hang-up, a way-gone ghost what's been wiggin' out."

I looked around. No ghosts showed their faces.

Cool Beans took a sip of the water and another bite of the sandwich.

"Well?" I said.

"Don't rush me, Rufus." The possum swung the sage in a circle. "By the powers of bebop and the rhymes of hip-hop, we release this uptight specter to the Land of Nod."

The temperature dropped. I hugged my arms. Natalie fluffed her feathers and surveyed the room.

Cool Beans shuffled in a herky-jerky dance step. "And now, I gum to the hi-fi's hum, a groovy tune to make this ghoulie melt. Shabbidy-wee-wop, skibbidy-do-bop, yeahhh!"

Eyes closed, he raised the burning bundle high and scatted some more nonsense syllables. The bongos rose to a crescendo.

The air seemed to shimmer. I felt a sudden rush of heat.

I glanced at Natalie. "Think it's working?"

"I don't know," she said. "But he did set the curtains on fire."

13

Let's Call the Whole Sing Off

Maureen DeBree was not amused. The mongoose custodian put out the flames and sent us packing. When Natalie and I returned for after-school rehearsal, the thick odor of scorched velvet filled the room.

Mr. Ratnose looked grim. Some of his whiskers were missing, and one eye twitched like a flickering stoplight. Still, he led our rehearsal.

I kept checking for ghostly signs. We got through the first song ("There Is Nothin' Like a Dane") in one piece. Then most of the cast worked on dances while I practiced Omlet's duel with LaSlurpie (played by Bjorn Freeh).

No spooks interfered.

The sword fight went well, I thought, but somehow my stick sword got stuck—up Bjorn's nose.

While removing it, I leaned in. "You know, I'm still looking for your twin," I said. "But I haven't had any luck."

"Don't—*ow!*—worry," said the anole lizard.

"But the phantom may have taken him. Aren't your parents frantic?"

Bjorn wiped his nose. "Nah, they hardly miss him."

Strange. My parents would've called out the army and navy by now.

We started sword fighting again—this time more carefully. Something occurred to me. "Hey, Bjorn," I said, clonking my stick against his.

"Yeah?" he said.

"I was wondering: How do your folks tell you and your brother apart?"

His stick thwacked mine. "Easy. I wear blue, he wears black."

I glanced down at his blue T-shirt and his stick slipped past my guard—*"Oof!"*—right into my gut.

Bjorn offered a fake-y smile. "Oops," he said. "Now we're even."

I rubbed my belly. There was more going on with this lizard than met the eye. But I didn't get the chance to find out what.

Most of the kids were still practicing their dance steps. Bjorn left, and Waldo, Boo Dinkum, and three kids playing grave diggers came onstage.

Boo was frostier than a snowman's undies. From the sidelines, his father glared at me like I'd stolen the last cockroach cupcake. As the musical humming-bird Zoomin' Mayta tickled the ivories, we sang the graveyard song.

> *"Alas, poor Yorick,*
> *You're really, really dead.*
> *There's nothing left behind you*
> *Except an empty head."*

Ms. Mayta had stopped us to correct a few sour notes when we all heard it: a high, eerie voice, singing the second verse.

"Alaaas, pooor Yorick, you bony, bony duuude..."

I scanned the room. The group onstage was struck dumb, and the dancers were otherwise occupied. Where was the singer hiding?

Something fluttered high above. I glanced up. Was it a trick of the light, or did a gleaming shape flit past? I blinked, and it had vanished.

So much for the exorcism.

"Why is everyone lollygagging about?" boomed

Mr. Ratnose. "Back to work, chop-chop. Let's see the grave-digger dance."

Halfheartedly, we clomped around the stage. I kept checking the ceiling for the shining figure's return.

Maybe that's why I missed the booby trap right in front of me.

Suddenly, my foot met no resistance. The stage gave way.

The board I'd stepped on seesawed up and whopped Boo Dinkum in the chops.

Klonk!

The chunky chipmunk tumbled back into the grave diggers, bowling them over like an all-star linebacker on a touchdown drive.

"Haw-ha—" My cackle was cut short when the same board completed its arc and bopped me on the head—*thonk!* I dropped beneath the stage like an overripe mango.

"*Umph!*" The belly flop took my breath away. Slowly, I sat up in the dark and felt my head. A throbbing knot was forming.

When Mr. Ratnose pried up the trick board, light streamed in. "Well?" he asked. "What have you learned in your investigation?"

"Teacher," I said, "something is definitely rotten in the state of Denver. And you can quote me on that."

14

Haunt for Red October

All weekend long, I racked my brains. This case was more tangled than a pair of pythons on a hot date. And the clues kept leading back to the ghost.

But how to catch a ghost? For three nights straight, Natalie and I stayed up late watching scary videos to see how the real ghostbusters did it. All we got were bloodshot eyes and popcorn-bloated bellies (not that there's anything wrong with that).

Monday and Tuesday flitted by like... well, ghosts. Still no plan. Opening night loomed like a truck in the rearview mirror.

The KOWS protesters got tougher with each rehearsal. We investigated them, along with our other suspects. Nothing solid. In my heart, I knew the phantom was our culprit.

Still, on Wednesday at lunch, Natalie and I revisited the soccer team. This time, my old playmate Buddy the badger was with them. Interesting.

He shot us a glare, but since we didn't seem to be detecting, he let it ride. Frankie the chuckwalla, on the other hand, twice sent the soccer ball whizzing at our skulls. We ducked.

"Do you think someone on the team is giving Buddy his orders?" asked Natalie.

I surveyed the chaos of their game. "From the looks of it, nobody's giving orders out there. Maybe the coach?..."

But the soccer coach was nowhere to be seen. When I asked Angie the weasel where her coach was, she sneered. "Not here."

"Well, *duh*," I said. "Tell me something I *don't* know."

She scratched an ear. "If a vulture is threatened, it can ralph up the entire contents of its stomach. How's that?"

I blinked. "Fascinating."

We decided to investigate the team another time.

From nowhere, Shirley Chameleon appeared at my side. "I just can't wait for tomorrow," she said, long tail curling.

"What's tomorrow?" I asked. "Your personality transplant?"

She giggled. "Opening night, silly. Mr. Ratnose said that's when we can start kissing for real." Shirley turned more shades of red than a sunset through smog.

I would've enjoyed the show if not for a feeling like gypsy moths were dive-bombing my stomach.

"Ugh... that's, uh, really... something," I choked out.

Natalie rescued me. "Come on, Chet. There's some important evidence you have to see." She took my elbow and towed me down the field.

"What evidence?" I asked.

"Evidently, you were about to undergo a cootie attack," she said.

"Thanks, partner. I owe you one."

She grinned. "You owe me a lot more than that. Think you can make it through the school day in one piece?"

I nodded. "Sure. If it's a piece of cake."

Somehow, the day passed. What can you say about classes? I came, I pretended to learn something, I left.

After school, Natalie and I met by the auditorium and watched the scene.

Like a bullfrog's throat on a hot summer night,

KOWS's numbers had swelled. I spotted Frankie, Angie, Buddy, and a bunch of their fellow soccer players. Even some debate-club nerds had joined in—hey, any excuse for a good spat.

My fellow actors pushed and shoved to break through their line. I was surprised by how physical some protesters were getting. "The play's the THING! We will be cancel*ING*!" they chanted.

Physical, but not very poetic.

Tensions were coming to a head like a zit pushing up from under the skin.

"Either this musical is going down in flames," I said, "or it'll be the biggest hit since the cafeteria started All-You-Can-Eat Pizza Day."

Natalie glanced over. "And either way, you're stuck with it."

"Thanks for reminding me, birdie."

She shrugged. "Shoot, that's what friends are for."

"Is *that* what they're for?" I said. "I always wondered."

15

Stress Rehearsal

Thursday tumbled in like a Gila monster in a dryer—hot, dizzy, and mean. Opening night, and still no Scott Freeh. I felt like the world's dumbest detective.

And soon I'd look like it, too—in my cheesy Omlet costume.

Our last rehearsal was a subdued affair. The cast listened to our director's spiel with all the pep and pizzazz of prisoners before a firing squad.

Mr. Ratnose showed the strain. Clumps of hair were missing from his head, his whiskers looked like he'd gotten a home perm from a blind mongoose, and now both eyes were twitching. But he was more stubborn than ever.

As we met by the stage, Waldo raised his paw. "Mr. Ratnose?" he said. "This play isn't fun anymore. Can I drop out?" Several students seconded the motion.

My teacher's gaze grew hot enough to melt diamonds. He turned it on the cast like the villain in the last scene of a bad sci-fi movie.

"Drop out?" he barked. *"Nobody* drops out. We open tonight, and this is dress rehearsal."

Bosco Rebbizi grimaced. "Does that mean I hafta wear a dress?" he said.

I would swear that steam came out of Mr. Ratnose's ears. But maybe I'd been chasing ghosts too long.

"Dress rehearsal," growled our teacher, "is when we add costumes and sets."

"Oh," said Bosco.

"Any other brilliant questions?"

After that, things settled down. We tried on our lame-o costumes, tights and all. Boo Dinkum was one of the few happy campers. The chipmunk preened and posed, asking everyone, "Doesn't this costume make me look slimmer?"

All I could think was, *How do I avoid Shirley's smooch?*

Just before the run-through began, the stagehands moved the sets into place. The opening music played. But just as we started to sing...

"Stop! Wait! Hold it right there!" cried Mr. Ratnose.

We held it. What was wrong?

With trembling finger, Mr. Ratnose indicated the set behind us. "Who is responsible for this travesty?"

I could've pointed out that a lot of folks were asking the same thing about his play. But I didn't.

"What's wrong?" I asked.

"That . . . *thing!*" he thundered.

We turned to see, and then the snickers started. On a portable wooden wall was painted a country scene: rolling green hills dotted with happy cows.

Nice enough, I guess. But what did it have to do with Omlet's castle?

"Ms. Petite!" hollered Mr. Ratnose.

The stylish ground squirrel sauntered out from backstage. "You called?"

"What is on that set?" said the fuming rat.

"Exactly what you asked my students to paint," she answered calmly, adjusting her scarf. "Omlet's cattle."

"I said *castle,* not *cattle.*"

Bona Petite shrugged. "My mistake. Your writing is hard to make out."

"I told you face-to-face," said Mr. Ratnose.

"Even so," she said.

My teacher grabbed his ears. For a second, I

thought he might rip them off. "Just...repaint it," he said, his voice shaking.

Ms. Petite glanced at her watch. "But the paint won't dry before we open."

Mr. Ratnose turned the most interesting shade of violet. I'd thought that only chameleons could manage that color. He sucked in some deep breaths.

"Very well," he snarled. "It stays. Everyone, take it from the top."

And so we lurched through our last rehearsal. Boo Dinkum's dad watched with the parent volunteers, a nasty grin on his ugly mug. I couldn't tell whether he was plotting mischief or enjoying the sheer awfulness of our play.

The performance passed in a blur of kick-turn-fight-sing. And then came my romantic duet with Shirley.

I sang: "Get thee to a nunnery. You'll find it much more funnery."

She crooned: "Omlet, you're my smoochie-pie. I'm yours until the day I die."

And suddenly, it was time. I cringed.

"Oh, Omlet, you're my sweet patootie."

Shirley grabbed my face and swung her puckered lips straight at mine!

No time to react. Her lips sped closer.

I closed my eyes.

Then—*ka-ronnnch!* The ceiling fell in.

My head and shoulders ached. My face was smooshed. If this was romance, it was for the birds.

A merciless weight pressed me into the floor, cutting off my air supply. I grew as dizzy as a second grader after a sackful of Halloween candy.

"Hwolp!" I tried to call. "Swumbuddy, hwolp!"

Muffled voices reached my ears. As if through a fog, I heard someone say, "One, two, three, heave!" And the world returned.

Someone flipped me over onto my back.

"Chet, are you all right?" Natalie's worried face popped into view. I raised my head. A bunch of kids were helping Mr. Ratnose push the set back into place. So that's what had fallen on me. I cleared my throat.

"Yes?" said Natalie.

"What time is it?" I croaked.

She glanced at the wall clock. "A little after eleven."

I nodded, and my head swam. Just four more hours till opening night. Plenty of time to solve a case and catch a bad guy before the curtain went up.

If I lived that long.

16

Hurtin' for Curtain

My bump on the noggin worked like a magic "get out of jail" card. The rest of the day, I just kicked back, free from class work and full of snacks.

If I'd known it would let me off the hook so well, I would've pulled this scam ages ago. Pain or no pain, I was smiling.

During quiet reading time, Mr. Ratnose visited my comfy pallet at the back of the classroom.

"Feeling better?" he asked.

"A little," I said, milking it.

"That's good." Mr. Ratnose poured a glass of soda pop. "Don't worry about finding whoever's harassing my play—just rest. We want you in tip-top shape for the performance."

My jaw dropped. "But I thought I wouldn't have to—"

He patted my shoulder and handed me the glass. "Don't be silly," he said. "You're the star. We couldn't do it without you."

"But—"

"Drink up." Mr. Ratnose offered a kindly grin, but his eyes were edged with iron. Then I knew: Not even death could get me out of doing this play.

Zero hour approached. The last bell rang, and the whole school headed for the auditorium. The KOWS protesters, sensing defeat, waved their signs halfheartedly. And when they thought no one was looking, they joined the crowd.

Parents and kids poured into the building like velvet-ant pancake batter onto a griddle. In a better world, I would've been home, eating those pancakes.

Instead, I slipped through the side door with the other actors and joined the backstage pandemonium.

Costume pieces fluttered through the air as parent volunteers tried to dress the kids. A porcupine from Natalie's class punctured his vest. Shirley and Bitty Chu squabbled over who got the pink dress. Tempers ran high.

The crew had packed the backstage with fake

swords, old-fashioned furniture, pillows, and all sorts of rubbish. I barked my shin on a gas canister.

"Yowie!"

"Careful!" said Bona Petite. She steadied the metal cylinder. "Are you hurt?"

"Me? Naw, I'm a lizard of steel," I said. "Hey, why the gas?"

"Our big finale," the elegant ground squirrel said. "Party balloons." She summoned a huge masked figure who looked vaguely familiar. "Move these canisters, will you?"

"Sure thing, Coach," said the creature in a high, thick voice. He lifted the cylinders and trundled off.

How classy. Leave it to Bona Petite to come up with a wonderful finish to what I suspected would be a less-than-wonderful play.

Figuring that a moving target is safest, I headed for the wings. If the parent volunteers didn't notice me, they couldn't make me wear tights.

But a hard paw seized my tail and dragged me back. It belonged to Boo Dinkum's dad.

"Here." The burly chipmunk thrust my costume into my hands. "Put this on. Or do you want me to do it for you?"

I squinted at him. If Mr. Dinkum had his way, I might be wearing the tights around my neck. "I've got it, thanks," I said.

He glared. "My boy can act rings around you."

"Ah, but can he dance 'La Cucaracha' while juggling kumquats and snorting milk out his nose?" I asked.

For a moment, the chipmunk's eyes narrowed, and something cold and mean peeked through. Then it was gone.

Mr. Dinkum mustered a fake smile. "Break a leg, Gecko. You and Boo are fellow thespians, after all."

I lifted my chin. "I can't speak for Boo, but I've never *thesp*ed in my life."

The chipmunk made a disgusted sound, then split. Natalie spoke from beside me: "A *thespian* is an actor."

I coughed. "I knew that."

She adjusted her queenly gown and nodded after Boo's father. "Think we should keep an eye on Mr. Sunshine?" she asked.

I studied the tangle of kids and parents backstage. "Definitely. I've got a bad feeling."

"Me, too," said Natalie. "This gown is too tight."

"Joke if you like, but keep your eyes peeled. We may have to act fast."

Mr. Ratnose clapped his hands and shushed the cast. We gathered in a rough circle, everyone clad in tights and funny feathered hats and velvet gowns.

We looked like a history book that had warped in the rain.

"Actors, parents, stage crew," said Mr. Ratnose, "lend me your ears. We come to praise Shakespeare, not to bury him."

I looked at Natalie. She lifted an eyebrow. Sometimes Mr. Ratnose was more ham than rat.

"Many have said this musical couldn't be done," he said. "And many have tried to stop us." He glared around the circle. "But here we are at last. Have a great show, and break a leg, everyone!"

I muttered to Natalie, "Why this obsession with leg breaking? Is this a Mafia production?"

My nervous castmates took their opening positions. Beyond the blue curtain, the crowd gabbled like a gang of penguins at a sushi bar.

I took a deep breath and could still smell the singed velvet. My heart thudded a ragged beat.

"The ghost isn't gonna like this," whispered Waldo.

"I'm scared," Bitty Chu whined.

Here goes nothing, I thought.

Zoomin' Mayta pounded out the opening chords. The curtains parted.

And the play began.

17

Stage Flight

Amazingly, we made it through the first couple of scenes. True, our singing sounded like a crow gargling with barbed wire, and our dancing looked like a water buffalo giving birth in a hurricane. But we got through it.

The audience clapped and grinned like they'd never seen anything more spectacular. Poor fools.

No sets fell, no goo dripped. Still, my nerves were strung tighter than a Chinese mandolin.

After my big scene with the guards, I was gathering my wits offstage.

Natalie approached. "See anything spooky?" she whispered.

"Besides this play?" I said.

We scanned the dimly lit backstage. Everything looked normal. (If you call it normal to see a ferret in tights and a cape.)

Onstage, Waldo the furball was singing to his character's son, LaSlurpie (played by Bjorn). If overacting was a crime, Bjorn would've been in the hoosegow for life.

"Neither a burrower nor a lender be," sang Waldo.

And then I caught the echo. A faint, eerie voice crooned, "Neeeither a burrower nor a lender beee."

Natalie heard it, too. We scanned the wings. And then a glimmer far above caught our eyes. The ghost!

I tapped Natalie's shoulder and pointed toward the ladder; we would creep up behind the phantom and surprise it. She nodded.

Quietly as an eighth grader returning from a midnight ramble, I eased up the ladder. Natalie flapped her way to the high catwalk.

Softly we crept. But we needn't have worried. Hunched over on the far end of the walk, the phantom was singing to itself, lost in its own world.

We were almost upon it now. The spook shone with a green and white phosphorescence. It looked like some shaggy beast made of light.

Just a step away, it struck me: What could we do against a ghost?

Too late.

The phantom turned. It saw us and uttered a low moan.

I think I may have moaned, too. What a sight!

The thing rose to its full height, looming above us. Huge eyes glared, a misshapen mouth snarled. It reached out a shining arm, and Natalie and I stepped back.

"What do you waaant?" it keened.

Natalie nudged me. I nudged her back.

"Welll?" said the phantom.

"Uh, we want you to return Scott Freeh," I said. "Um, please?"

"Whaaat?" said the ghost. It reared up.

We backed away a few more steps.

"And pretty please, stop, er, disrupting the play?" asked Natalie.

The glowing shape swayed toward us. I tensed, ready for a quick getaway.

"How daaare you accuuuse me!" it rumbled.

I hissed to Natalie, "Maybe this wasn't such a great idea."

"Now you tell me," she whispered back.

Then the ghost surprised me. "I looove plaaays," it said softly. "I would neeever interfere. And whooo is this Scott of whooom you speak?"

"The lizard you kidnapped," I said, clenching my fists. "Don't try your mumbo jumbo with me."

"*Shhh,*" the ghost said. It pointed to the stage below. "They're aaacting."

I glanced down. I guess you could call it acting. Waldo's scene was ending; Rosenblatz and Gildyfern's soft-shoe dance came next. I would have to join them soon.

"What about Shirley's disappearance and the threatening notes?" I asked.

"Yeah, and the booby-trapped stage and falling set?" said Natalie.

"That wasn't meee," said the phantom. "I ooonly watch and sing."

"Oh yeah?" I said, feeling bolder. "What about the time it rained slime?"

The ghost looked up. "Sooorry," it said. "I got exciiited."

I eased closer. The smell of moldy bath mats and bottled moonshine met me. "Then who's sabotaging this play?" I asked. "Who's the culprit?"

The creature sighed. "I ooonly saw it from behiiind," it said.

"What did it look like?" asked Natalie.

"Brooown fur."

"Tail?" I asked.

"Yeeessss," said the ghost.

I shook my head. "No, ectoplasm-for-brains. I mean long or short? Striped or plain?"

"Looong. And it haaad a skinny lizaaard to help."
The ghost swung its head toward the stage. "Say,
wasn't that your cuuue?"

Below, I heard Rosenblatz say, "Golly, where is
that Omlet? Om-*let*!"

I grabbed the curtain and prepared to slide down.
The phantom put a paw cold as katydid Popsicles on
my arm.

"They will striiike agaaain," said the spook. "I
heard them taaalking."

"What did they say?" I asked.

"'Ooopening night, we'll haaave the last
laaaugh.'"

Gildyfern's voice reached me. "You say you're
looking for OMLET? I WONDER WHERE HE
IS."

"Go!" Natalie hissed.

She would have to finish up with the ghost. Time
for my big entrance.

As I slid down the curtains, she asked the spirit,
"Who were you, anyway?"

Its faint response came: "Emerson Hiiicky. I
founded this schoool."

Great. We'd had a haunted cafeteria all along?
That explained some of the school lunches.

Then I hit the stage. "What ho, dude-ios?" I said.
And we were back into the play.

I listened to Rosenblatz's response and glanced to the right. Just at the edge of the audience stood the chipmunk Mr. Dinkum.

He was brown-furred. And long-tailed.

And his grin was positively evil.

18

Room and Sword

All the time I was singing "Alas, Poor Yorick" with the grave diggers, my mind raced. How did Mr. Dinkum and his lizard helper plan to get the "last laugh" on us? And how could I warn Mr. Ratnose while I was stuck onstage?

My teacher stood in the wings, tapping a foot and singing along. I caught his eye and jerked my head toward Mr. Dinkum.

Mr. Ratnose nodded and smiled.

I shook my head and gazed meaningfully at the evil chipmunk.

"Eyes front," Mr. Ratnose mouthed.

I rolled my eyes. At the end of the song, I checked the spot where Mr. Dinkum had stood. He was gone.

Boo was in the next scene. As we recited our lines, I kept watching the backstage wings for a rogue chipmunk. Mr. Dinkum wouldn't sabotage the play while his own son was onstage. Would he?

"What's your sneaky father up to?" I whispered to Boo.

"Fair Omlet," he said loudly, "methinks you have flipped your wig." Boo glared. *Duh.* I shouldn't have expected a straight answer from this chipmunk.

The play rolled on. My sword fight with Bjorn Freeh was next.

We thwacked our fake swords against each other, and I noticed the anole lizard struck even harder than before. What was *his* problem? While we fought, I sweated over how to let someone know about Mr. Dinkum.

Natalie appeared in the wings, just offstage. Perfect. I retreated toward her, and Bjorn followed, clacking away with his sword.

"Natalie!" I hissed. "It's Mr. Dinkum! Brown fur, long tail."

She nodded. "I'm on it."

Bjorn's sword crunched down on my knuckles.

"Ow!" I said. "I mean . . . uh, forsooth!"

The lizard's eyes glittered. I frowned. Something was off here.

"Are you mixed up in Mr. Dinkum's plot?" I whispered, slashing at Bjorn until he stepped back.

Clink! Clank!

"That loser?" he hissed. "Why would I plot with him when Coach has a much better plan?" Bjorn drove me back with mighty thrusts.

Clink! Clank! Clonk!

Odd. Bjorn had grown stronger. He hadn't been that skilled a sword fighter in rehearsals....

I blocked his thrust. "Take that, LaSlurpie!" I cried. Then, whispering: "*Coach* has a better plan? But you're not on a team."

Bjorn grinned. He swung his long tail in an arc, sweeping my feet out from under me. "Thou ist scrambled, young Omlet," he cried.

"Oof!" I fell, hard.

Maybe the impact jarred my brain. Or maybe it was the sight of a masked lizard in a blue T-shirt standing on the sidelines with a gas canister. A lizard that looked just like Bjorn.

The sword slashed straight at my head. I blocked it, then hooked my tail around my attacker's ankle.

"You're not Bjorn," I whispered, yanking hard. "You're Scott Freeh!"

Whump! The faker hit the floor. "That's right," said Scott, "for all the good it'll do you . . ."

He had a point. I was stuck onstage until the end of the play. By then, the soccer coach would've pulled his prank.

Hiram the toad entered as King Gaudiest. "Now, now, youngsters," he croaked. "Put up thy swords and be friends."

Natalie, in queenly robes, joined him. "Boys will be boys, *tra-la.*"

While the king and queen pulled us to our feet and made us shake hands, my poor overworked brain puzzled.

"Natalie," I muttered, "it's not Mr. Dinkum; it's the soccer coach."

"But . . ." She glanced at the wings, where Mr. Ratnose and Boo's dad argued in whispers. "Then who's the soccer coach?" she mumbled.

That, as the real Hamlet once said, was the question. Half my brain wrestled with it while half tried to remember my goofy lines.

Then Shirley Chameleon flounced onstage for our romantic duet.

My breath stopped. My lines fled like second graders in a game of tag.

"Prithee, my lord," said Shirley. "What's on thy mind?"

"Uh..." My mind was blank as a blackboard in summertime. "That is..."

"Thoughts of love," hissed Shirley. "That's your line."

"Thoughts of love," I said, "and, um..."

My eyes searched the audience like I'd find the words written there. In the tense silence, some folks coughed. Others winced in sympathy.

I noticed the real Bjorn and the masked bruiser I'd seen earlier—both standing in the aisles with gas canisters.

That bruiser looked so familiar. Then he scratched his belly with claws like swords, and I knew him: Buddy the badger, big as life.

"Let us sing, good Omlet," said Shirley. She gestured frantically at Ms. Mayta, who plonked out the chords on the piano.

As we sang, my mind replayed an earlier scene.

But not from the musical. It was Buddy, carrying a canister, saying, "Sure thing, Coach."

Shirley scooted closer, ready for our big kiss.

My wits raced like a centipede on a hot plate. The pieces were coming together.

Buddy was a soccer player. So was Scott.

And their coach? She was a brown-furred, long-tailed squirrel named . . .

Bona Petite!

19

A Laugh-Baked Idea

For the next few minutes, everything seemed to happen at once, as if on a bank of TVs tuned to different nightmares. Shirley sang her last line and puckered up.

Without thinking, I grabbed the nearest actor, Boo Dinkum.

"Huh?" he said.

"You wanted this role," I said.

I shoved Boo into my place. In the mother of all kisses, Shirley Chameleon's cootie-filled lips smooched his.

Her eyes blinked open. *"What?!"* she squawked.

"Uh, sweet Azalea," I said, "you don't love me; you love my pal, um . . . Oratio, here. Be happy and have lots of babies!"

And with that, I dashed to the edge of the stage. But I was too late.

Buddy and Bjorn unscrewed the tops of their gas canisters and rolled the cylinders down the aisles. *Dang!* Clouds of gas spread through the audience.

"Mr. Ratnose!" I shouted.

Someone tittered.

Mr. Ratnose glared at me from the wings. I strode over and grabbed his arm. Natalie took his other arm, and we towed my teacher onstage, heels dragging.

Giggles rose from the crowd.

"Uh, prithee, good Earl of Ratnose," said Natalie. "We have uncovered a plot against the kingdom."

"Er, what?" said Mr. Ratnose, torn between anger and concern.

I saw where Natalie was going with this.

"Yeah," I said, eyeballing the room. "And the chief plot-a-teer is none other than...Baroness Bona Petite." I pointed at the ground squirrel. "She's trying to poison the whole kingdom!"

The audience busted a gut. Some were laughing so hard that tears ran.

I looked at Natalie. These folks were in mortal danger. What was so funny?

She raised her eyebrows and shook her head.

Bona Petite slipped a gas mask over her mocking smirk.

Then the canisters hit the foot of the stage, and we found out why she smiled. Ms. Petite had dosed the auditorium with laughing gas!

"Somebody—*ha, ha*—hold her," called Mr. Ratnose.

A chuckling Cool Beans and two giddy teachers blocked the doors.

The crowd roared. Parents pounded on the seats. Even Principal Zero smiled.

Bona Petite raced around the big room. No way out.

"Ms. Pet—*hee, hee*—ite tried to—*ha*—disrupt this play," I said, giggling. I leaned on Natalie for support. "She even—*ho, ho, ho*—kidnapped, threatened, and—*ha, ha, haw*—hurt students."

"And—*hee, hee*—he's not just joking!" Natalie cackled.

Principal Zero, the massive tomcat, rose unsteadily to his feet. "This is a—*ha, ha, ha*—a very serious—*hee*—charge," he chuckled. "The teachers' union will wa—*ha, ha*—want to know about this."

Ms. Petite jumped onstage. "This is no crime!" she shouted through her gas mask. "The crime took place when you chose this moron's lousy play"—she pointed at Mr. Ratnose—"over mine!"

"I—*ho, ho*—resent that," said the lean rat. He bent, hands on knees.

"Anyway, you'll never catch me," said Bona Petite. She dashed for the backstage exit. "I'm bound for Broadway!"

Through tears, I watched her run. She was right. Crippled with laughter, the cast was powerless to prevent her escape.

"Sto—*ha, ha*—op her!" I yelled.

The ground squirrel was just inches away from freedom.

Then, in a dizzying whoosh, a glowing shape swooped from the wings and scooped her up. The ghost!

It lifted Ms. Petite into the air and held her suspended above the stage.

"Youuu impersonaaated a phantom," the spook boomed. "I'll scaaare some sense into yooou!"

Like a psycho roller coaster, it dipped, swerved, and spun through the air. The unfortunate ground squirrel shrieked.

"Look!" said Natalie. "It's the—*hee*—ghost of Omlet's fa—*ha, ha*—ther. My dead husband."

Guffaws rocked the auditorium.

The ghost dropped a dizzy Bona Petite into the arms of our principal. Cackling, Mr. Zero and Cool Beans led Ms. Petite away. She wasn't smiling.

The audience leaped to their feet—those members who could stand, anyway. They cheered and chuckled and clapped. The cast took bow after bow.

Or maybe we were just doubled over with laughter.

20

Footloose and Phantom-Free

It took a while for the effects of the laughing gas to wear off. When it did, we sat on the stage, weak and loopy as a bundle of wet spaghetti.

Parents kept coming by. They complimented Mr. Ratnose until his ears turned pink. A sleek mink said, "Marvelous. I've never laughed so hard. What an exhilarating ending!"

"Superb!" raved a stout hedgehog. "And the special effects were stunning. I mean, that ghost!"

At that, Mr. Ratnose sent a suspicious look at Natalie and me. I gave him my best *who, me?* expression in return.

"I don't think we'll be seeing any more of that ghost," muttered Natalie.

"Why not?" I said.

She smoothed a wing feather. "Remember what Cool Beans said? That ghosts haunt because of unfinished business?"

"Yeah, so?"

"The ghost of Emerson Hicky told me he'd always wanted to be in a school play but died before he got the chance."

"Well, whaddaya know?" I clapped her on the back. "You're a ghostbuster."

"Just as I ex-spectered." She cackled.

I groaned.

Before they left for Principal Zero's office, Mr. Ratnose wormed the truth out of the Freeh twins and Buddy the badger. It seems Ms. Petite had charmed them all, as only a glamour-puss can do.

At her command, they had faked Scott's disappearance, rigged various booby traps, written phantom notes—even organized the KOWS protests. And with the aid of Ms. Petite's stage magic and smoke bombs, they'd rigged Shirley's dramatic reappearance.

"But why?" asked Mr. Ratnose.

Buddy looked down. "Dude, she's so *pretty,*" he said. "Who could say no?"

Natalie and I stood by the door and watched them go to meet their well-deserved punishment.

The spanking machine would need a tune-up after this.

Shirley Chameleon came simpering up. "Chet?" she said.

I coughed. "Sorry about wrecking our scene, sister. But with a private eye, the case comes first."

She batted her big green peepers. "Don't be silly," she said. "You saved the day, and you caught the culprit. I'd say you deserve a reward."

I turned to Natalie. "A horsefly burrito would hit the spot about now."

Shirley said, "I was thinking maybe..."

I turned back, and she smooched my cheek with a loud, cootie-licious smack!

Yuck!

"Chet Gecko, you're the best," said Shirley. And she sauntered away.

I wiped my cheek. Dames. Even when they're right, they're too much.

Natalie smirked. "Didn't look like you were struggling that hard."

"Partner," I said, "if that's the case, I'm a better actor than you thought."

We strolled out into the parking lot. The light of the afternoon sun had dipped everything in butterscotch. *Mmm, butterscotch...* I made plans for a pre-dinner treat.

Before climbing into our parents' waiting cars, Natalie and I paused.

"So, acting in a play wasn't too bad, was it?" she said.

"No worse than being nibbled to death by nematodes."

Natalie's eyes grew wide. "Ooh, what if they make a movie out of it? Who would you want to play you?"

"Sister," I said, "there's only one Chet Gecko. And I don't think I could go through that case a second time."

As we said good night, I reflected. Tomorrow would bring a new case. But that was all right. If my stint in show business had taught me anything, it was this: No matter what happens, the sleuth must go on.

Will Chet suffer a partner-ectomy?
Find out in
Murder, My Tweet

Lunch period found me cornered by Anne Gwish, a client who put the *koo* in *cuckoo*—and she was a parakeet.

"What?!" she squawked. "You let T-Bone *see* you? How on *earth* can you tail him now?"

"Well, I—"

Anne waved her wings. "Of all the sloppy, smart-mouthed, jelly-bellied—"

"You forgot lazy."

"Why, you can't even follow my boyfriend without getting spotted. Now I'll *never* know if T-Bone is two-timing me." She started plucking out her feathers.

I held out my palms in a calming gesture. "My partner Natalie is shadowing T-Bone. When we know something, you'll be the first to know."

The parakeet sneered. "Oh, like that makes sense," she said. "How can *I* be the first to know if *you* already know it?"

I clenched my fists and sucked in a deep breath. Mom always said to count to ten when I got steamed, but with this dizzy dame, it might take a hundred. (And math has never been my strong point.)

"Chet! Chet!" My partner's voice was as welcome as a jumbo cricket Slurpee after a ten-day trek around the sun. Natalie flapped pell-mell across the playground, straight toward us.

"Ah, there she is now," I said to Anne. "Relax. Everything is fine."

Natalie skidded to a landing. "Oh, Chet—something awful!" She panted.

"I knew it," snapped Anne Gwish, giving me a sharp, I-told-you-so look.

I ignored her. "Natalie, you remember our *client,* Anne," I said, hoping my partner would take the hint and cool it in front of our customer.

She didn't. "The worst thing has happened. You'll never believe . . . ," she said.

I gave up. "What?"

"I'm suspended from school!"

"Huh? You don't have to go to school?" I scratched my head. "I thought you said it was something awful."

"It *is,*" Natalie moaned.

She was serious. The crazy mockingbird actually enjoyed schoolwork, strange as that may seem.

Anne Gwish pecked my arm. "She's *suspended*?" said the parakeet. "What kind of—"

I brushed her off. "Button up, you," I said, and turned back to Natalie. "Hey, it's not so bad. You'll be a soap-opera queen, just like your mom."

"Chet, it's not funny. I can't come to school. They won't even let me work on cases with you."

"*What?*" I rocked back on my tail. "You're right, that's not funny. How could they suspend you? You're Miss Straight-A's-For-Days."

"That's *Ms.* Straight-A's-For-Days," she said. "And Vice Principal Shrewer accused me of blackmail."

I stared, mouth gaping. This made about as much sense as my bogus science report on the sand dolphins of the Kalahari Desert.

"*Blackmail?*" I said.

Anne butted her green head into my shoulder. "She's a *blackmailer?*" she said.

I butted back. "Park it and lock it, cheese-beak."

Tears trembled in Natalie's eyes. Her mouth quivered. "Chet, I didn't do it."

"Of course not," I said. "But why does Ms. Shrewer think you did?"

"Well, I was tailing T-Bone, and I dunno . . . maybe he spotted me . . ."

"He—*mmf!*" Anne tried to interrupt, but a firm hand around her beak put a stop to that.

Natalie hopped in agitation. "T-Bone dropped some kind of letter outside the vice principal's door. Ms. Shrewer caught me picking it up, and then she—"

"Aha! There's the blackmailer," a tight voice snapped. It was a no-nonsense shrew, Vice Principal Shrewer, with Principal Zero close behind her. "Come along, missy," she said. "I want you off this campus *now*."

Both of them clamped a paw onto Natalie's shoulder and started to lead her away. Natalie twisted to look back at me.

"You've got to clear my name, Chet. Hurry!"

Ms. Shrewer spun Natalie's head to the front. And just like that, they marched her off.

"*Mmf! Mgmng mmf!*"

What was that sound? A mutant mole with a speech impediment?

Turning, I found that my hand still gripped Anne's beak. I released it.

"And what have you got to say for yourself?" I said. "What's so important that it couldn't wait until after my partner got kicked out of school?"

"You," she hissed, "are fired."

I shook my head. Where had I heard that one before?

Look for more mysteries from the Tattered Casebook of Chet Gecko in hardcover and paperback

Case #1 *The Chameleon Wore Chartreuse*

Some cases start rough, some cases start easy. This one started with a dame. (That's what we private eyes call a girl.) She was cute and green and scaly. She looked like trouble and smelled like . . . grasshoppers.

Shirley Chameleon came to me when her little brother, Billy, turned up missing. (I suspect she also came to spread cooties, but that's another story.) She turned on the tears. She promised me some stinkbug pie. I said I'd find the brat.

But when his trail led to a certain stinky-breathed, bad-tempered, jumbo-sized Gila monster, I thought I'd bitten off more than I could chew. Worse, I had to chew fast: If I didn't find Billy in time, it would be bye-bye, stinkbug pie.

Case #2 *The Mystery of Mr. Nice*

How would you know if some criminal mastermind tried to impersonate your principal? My first clue: He was nice to me.

This fiend tried everything—flattery, friendship, food—but he still couldn't keep me off the case. Natalie and I followed a trail of clues as thin as the cheese on a cafeteria hamburger. And we found a ring of corruption that went from the janitor right up to Mr. Big.

In the nick of time, we rescued Principal Zero and busted up the PTA meeting, putting a stop to the evil genius. And what thanks did we get? Just the usual. A cold handshake and a warm soda.

But that's all in a day's work for a private eye.

Case #3 *Farewell, My Lunchbag*

If danger is my business, then dinner is my passion. I'll take any case if the pay is right. And what pay could be better than Mothloaf Surprise?

At least that's what I thought. But in this particular case, I bit off more than I could chew.

Cafeteria lady Mrs. Bagoong hired me to track down whoever was stealing her food supplies. The long, slimy trail led too close to my own backyard for comfort.

And much, much too close to my old archenemy, Jimmy "King" Cobra. Without the help of Natalie Attired and our school janitor, Maureen DeBree, I would've been gecko sushi.

Case #4 *The Big Nap*

My grades were lower than a salamander's slippers, and my bank account was trying to crawl under a duck's belly. So why did I take a case that didn't pay anything?

Put it this way: Would *you* stand by and watch some

evil power turn *your* classmates into hypnotized zombies? (If that wasn't just what normally happened to them in math class, I mean.)

My investigations revealed a plot meaner than a roomful of rhinos with diaper rash.

Someone at Emerson Hicky was using a sinister video game to put more and more students into la-la-land. And it was up to me to stop it, pronto—before that someone caught up with me, and I found myself taking the Big Nap.

Case #5   *The Hamster of the Baskervilles*

Elementary school is a wild place. But this was ridiculous.

Someone—or some*thing*—was tearing up Emerson Hicky. Classrooms were trashed. Walls were gnawed. Mysterious tunnels riddled the playground like worm chunks in a pan of earthworm lasagna.

But nobody could spot the culprit, let alone catch him.

I don't believe in the supernatural. My idea of voodoo is my mom's cockroach-ripple ice cream.

Then, a teacher reported seeing a monster on full-moon night, and I got the call.

At the end of a twisted trail of clues, I had to answer the burning question: Was it a vicious, supernatural were-hamster on the loose, or just another Science Fair project gone wrong?

Case #6   *This Gum for Hire*

Never thought I'd see the day when one of my worst enemies would hire me for a case. Herman the Gila Monster was a sixth-grade hoodlum with a first-rate left hook. He told me someone was disappearing the football team, and he had to put a stop to it. *Big whoop.*

He told me he was being blamed for the kidnappings, and he had to clear his name. *Boo hoo.*

Then he said that I could either take the case and earn a nice reward, or have my face rearranged like a bargain-basement Picasso painted by a spastic chimp.

I took the case.

But before I could find the kidnapper, I had to go undercover. And that meant facing something that scared me worse than a chorus line of criminals in steel-toed boots: P.E. class.

Case #7   *The Malted Falcon*

It was tall, dark, and chocolatey—the stuff dreams are made of. It was a treat so titanic that nobody had been able to finish one single-handedly (or even single-mouthedly). It was the Malted Falcon.

How far would you go for the ultimate dessert? Somebody went too far, and that's where I came in.

The local sweets shop held a contest. The prize: a year's supply of free Malted Falcons. Some lucky kid scored the winning ticket. She brought it to school for show-and-tell.

But after she showed it, somebody swiped it. And no one would tell where it went.

Following a strong hunch and an even stronger sweet tooth, I tracked the ticket through a web of lies more tangled than a rattlesnake doing the rumba. But the time to claim the prize was fast approaching. Would the villain get the sweet treat—or his just desserts?

Case #8   *Trouble Is My Beeswax*

Okay, I confess. When test time rolls around, I'm as tempted as the next lizard to let my eyeballs do the walking . . . to my neighbor's paper.

But Mrs. Gecko didn't raise no cheaters. (Some language manglers, perhaps.) So when a routine investigation uncovered a test-cheating ring at Emerson Hicky, I gave myself a new case: Put the cheaters out of business.

Easier said than done. Those double-dealers were slicker than a frog's fanny and twice as slimy.

Oh, and there was one other small problem: The finger of suspicion pointed to two dames. The ringleader was either the glamorous Lacey Vail, or my own classmate Shirley Chameleon.

Sheesh. The only thing I hate worse than an empty Pillbug Crunch wrapper is a case full of dizzy dames.